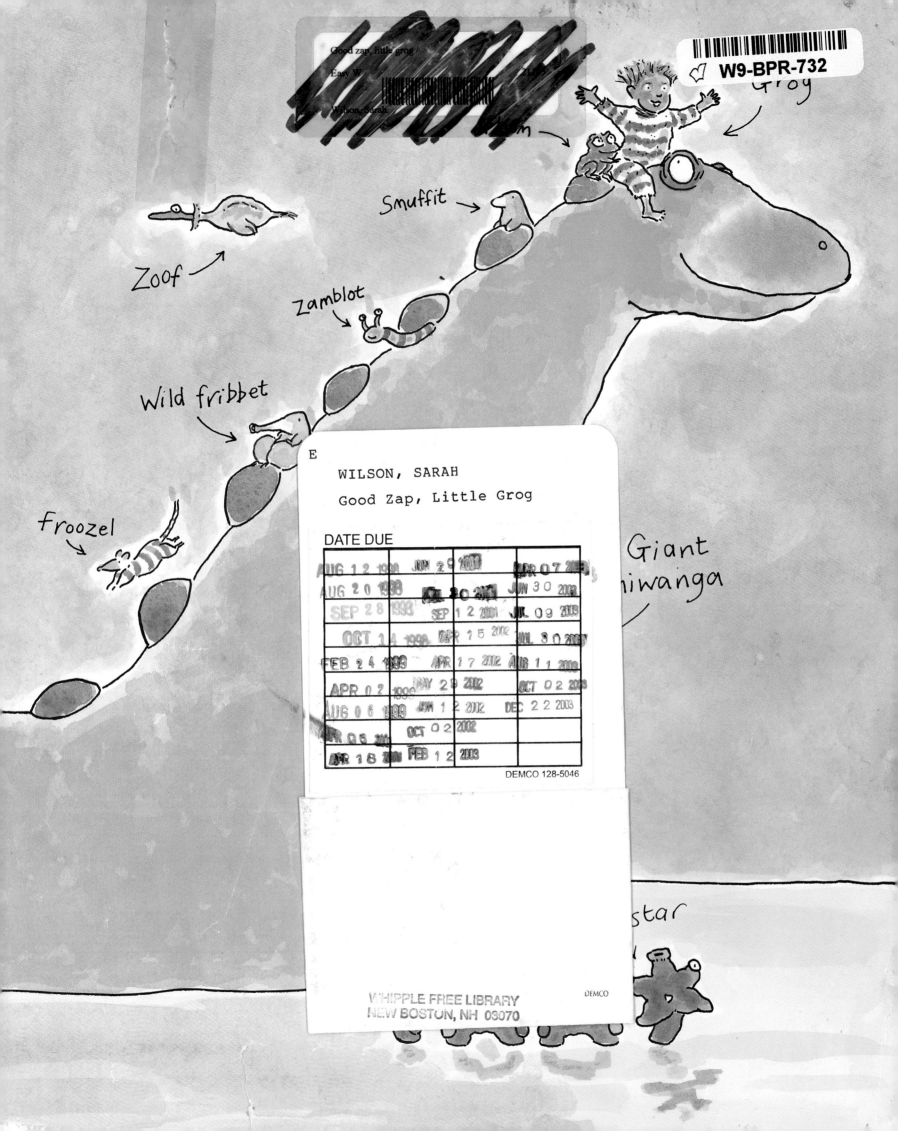

For Herb, with hugs
S.W.

For Niko
S.M.

Text copyright © 1995 by Sarah Wilson
Illustrations copyright © 1995 by Susan Meddaugh

All rights reserved.
First edition 1995

Library of Congress Cataloging-in-Publication Data

Wilson, Sarah.
Good zap, little grog / Sarah Wilson ; illustrated by Susan Meddaugh.—1st ed.
Summary: A fanciful depiction of a day in the life of little Grog.
ISBN 1-56402-286-2
[1. Fantasy. 2. Stories in rhyme.]
I. Meddaugh, Susan, ill.   II. Title.
PZ8.3.W698Go   1995   94-25700
[E]—dc20

10 9 8 7 6 5 4 3 2 1

Printed in Italy

This book has been typeset in Little Grog.
The pictures in this book were done in ink and watercolor.

Candlewick Press
2067 Massachusetts Avenue
Cambridge, Massachusetts 02140

GOOD ZAP, LITTLE GROG

illustrated by
Susan Meddaugh

Sarah Wilson

CANDLEWICK PRESS
CAMBRIDGE, MASSACHUSETTS

ZOODLE OOP

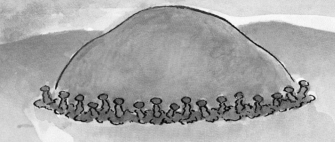

Zoodle oop, little Grog,
give a hug; stretch and yawn.
The night moons are fading.
There's shine on the lawn.

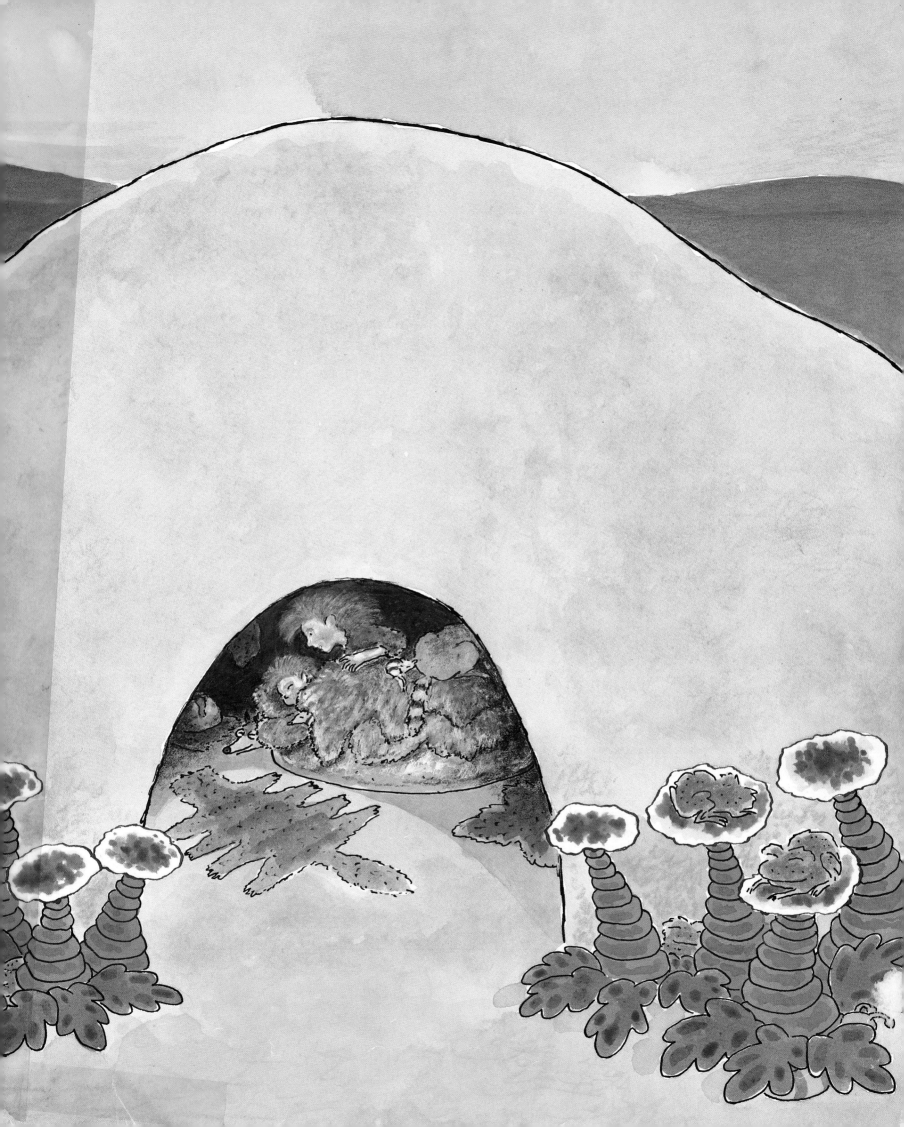

Uncurl from your covers,
you sleepy gurraff.
The ooglets are tuzzling.
(Try hard not to laugh!)

The flooms in the garden
have started to wink.
A tiny paroobie
is churling,
"Zlink-zlink!"

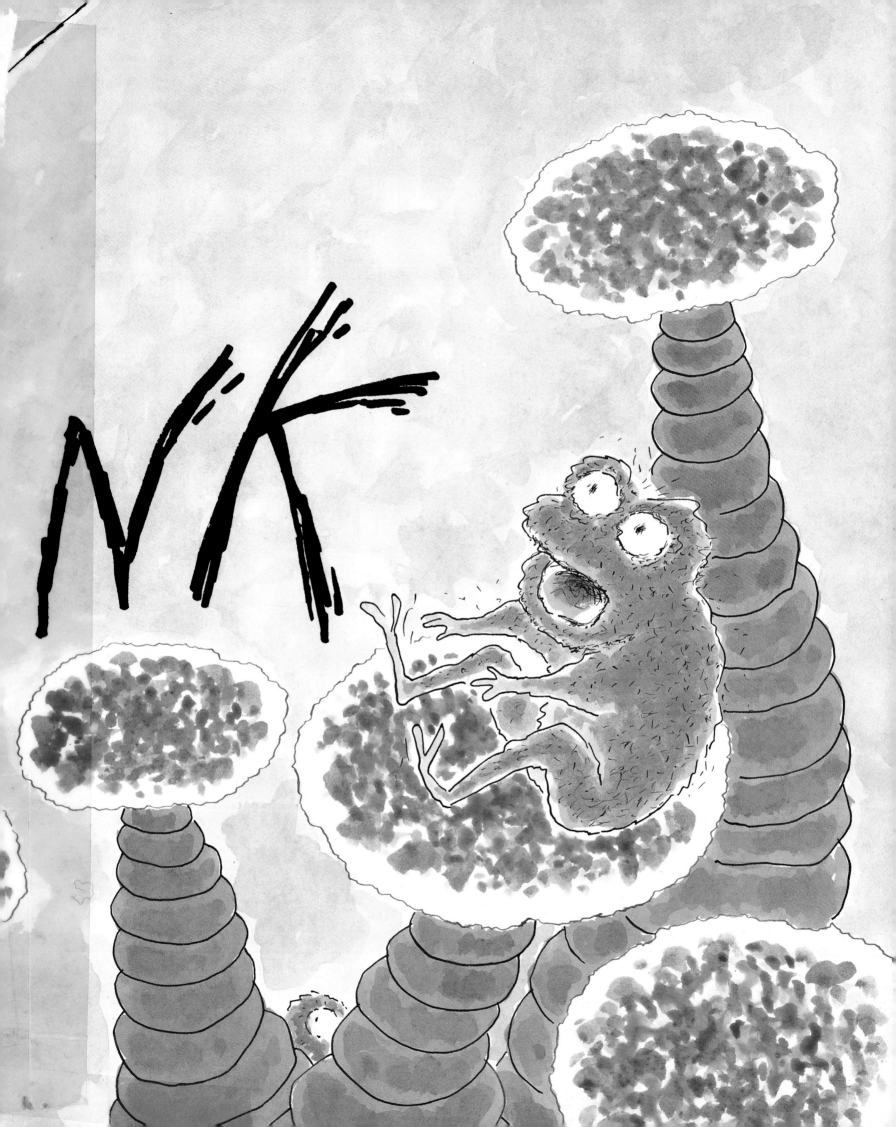

So hop to your glockers
and socks right away.
Zoodle oop, little Grog.

Run and play!
Run and play!

YOOP DOOZ

Yoop dooz, little Grog,
there are zoofs in the sky.
The glipneeps are jumping
and ready to fly.

The day-stars are fizzing
in polka-dot trails.
Your smibblets are giggling
and chasing their tails.

Nearby in the garden,
who's frilling for you?
A little green zibblet
in spangles—that's who!

So trok with the frullops
and chase every sun.
Yoop dooz,
little Grog.

Come have fun!
Come have fun!

GOOD ZAP

Good zap, little Grog,
the moons have turned pink.
The giant chiwangas
are starting to sink.

In the dusk of the garden
a wild fribbet humms,
and all the blue zamblots
are covered in flumms.

So wave to the smuffits
and bring in your grib.
In your soft, furry nightclothes,
bounce into your crib.

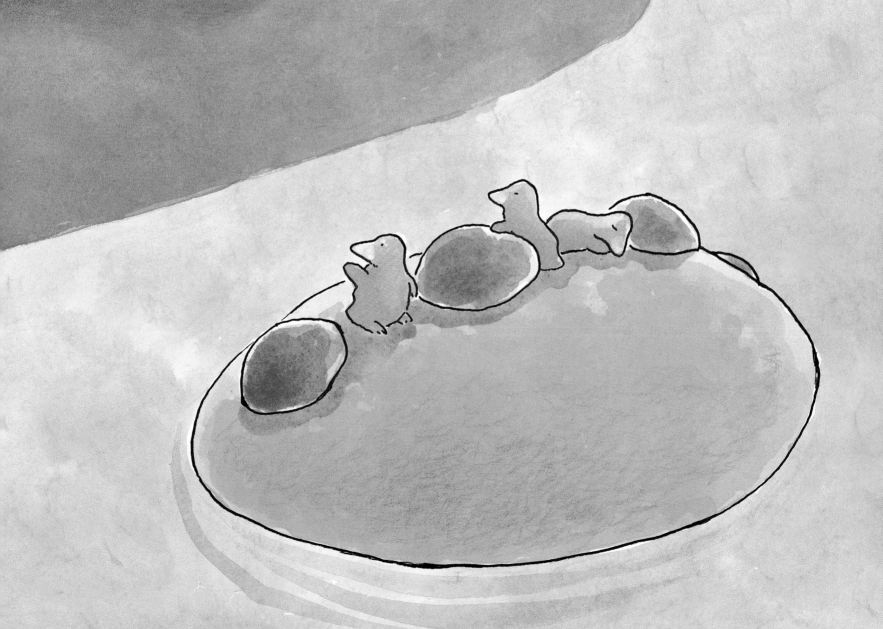

Now dream with the froozels
and snuggle your feet.
Good zap, little Grog.

Go to sleep.
Go to sleep.

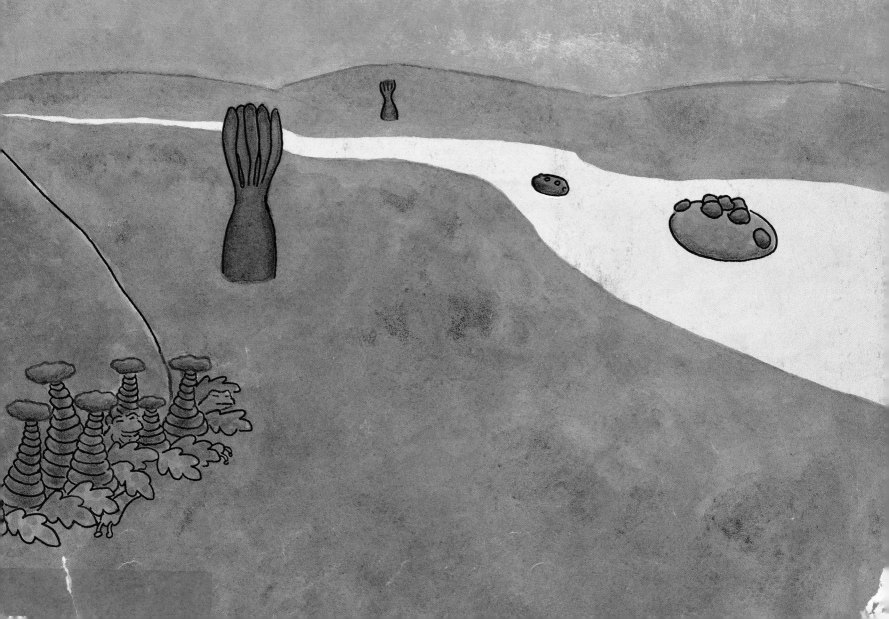